Four Winds Press
Macmillan Publishing Company
866 Third Avenue, New York, NY 10022
Collier Macmillan Canada, Inc.

Printed in Portugal by Resopal

10   9   8   7   6   5   4   3   2

The Library of Congress has cataloged this work as follows:

Gretz, Susanna.
   Teddy bears cure a cold / Susanna Gretz, Alison Sage. — 1st
American ed. — New York : Four Winds Press, 1984.

   [32] p. : col. ill. ; 23 x 26 cm.

   Summary: When William's cold seems to be lingering too long
and his demands for attention increase, the other teddy bears
work a miraculous cure.
   ISBN 0-02-736960-9

   1. Children's stories, English.   [1. Teddy Bears—Fiction.   2. Toys—
Fiction.   3. Sick—Fiction]   I. Sage, Alison.   II. Title.

PZ8.9.G917 Tc   1984   [E]dc19   84-4015
                            AACR 2   MARC

Library of Congress   AC

susanna gretz · alison sage

teddy bears
cure a cold

FOUR WINDS PRESS
New York

"I feel sick," said William.
"You can't be sick," said Andrew;
"we're going to try out our new tools."

"But I *am* sick,"
said William,
"and I am going to bed."

William did not eat his breakfast.

"Maybe he really is sick," said Robert.
"Don't believe it," said Louise;
"he just wants breakfast in bed."
"Let's go see," said Charles.

"You don't look so sick to me," said Louise.
"My throat hurts," William complained.

That afternoon, William was still in bed.
"Let's play monkey in the middle,"
said Andrew. "It will cheer you up."
"My head hurts," said William.

The next morning, Charles made William
a special breakfast.
"I'm not hungry," said William.
"William is always hungry,"
whispered Louise.
"He *must* be sick."

Charles found a thermometer.
Louise took out her flashlight.
"William, you have white spots
on your throat," she said.
"And he has a temperature, too," said Charles.
"We'll have to take good care of him."

Louise and John made the bed.
Robert found a hot-water bottle.
"I'll be in charge of the temperature
chart," said Charles.
Andrew made a honey-and-lemon drink.
"Thank you," croaked William.

That evening,
William felt worse.
One minute
he was hot;
the next minute
he was cold.
His sheets were sticky
and talking gave him
a headache.
The other bears tiptoed
away, and William
finally fell asleep.

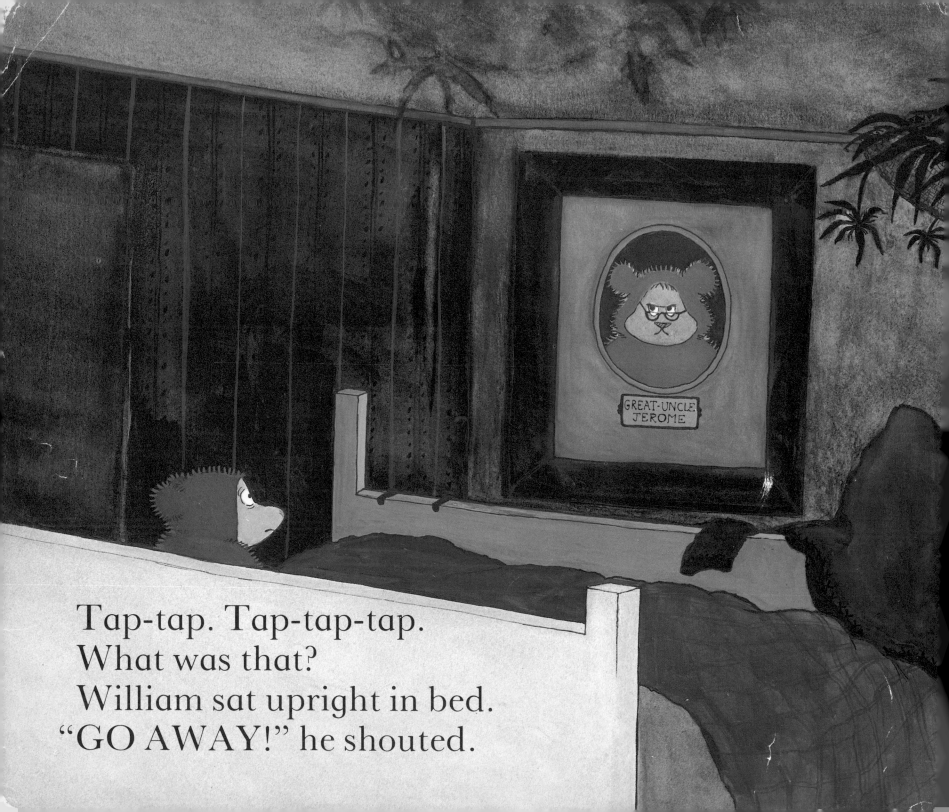

Tap-tap. Tap-tap-tap.
What was that?
William sat upright in bed.
"GO AWAY!" he shouted.

The light went on.
"I heard something tapping," said William.
"It must have been the wind," said Robert.
"And I *saw* things," said William.
"It's because you're sick," said Charles.

The next day,
there was a chocolate pig for William,
and Sara brought him some flowers.
"I hope you like tulips," she said.
Charles gave him a bell.
"Ring if you need anything," he said.
"Thank you," said William;
and for the next few days
he stayed in bed.

Then one morning, Sara made him some oatmeal.
"Thank you," said William.
"But could you make me a banana milkshake?"

Robert brought him
some apples.
"Thank you,"
said William;
"but will you
peel one for me?"

Andrew brought him some cards.
"Thank you," said William.
"But I'd rather have a new jigsaw puzzle . . .
and a bag of peanuts."
"Hmm," said Louise.

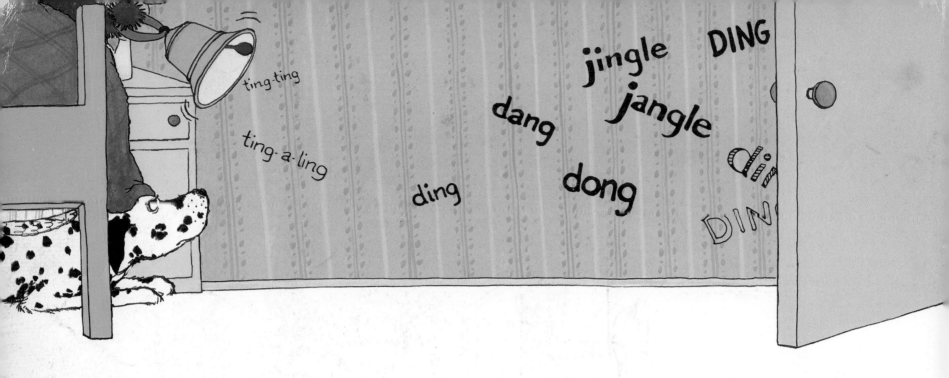

ting-ting

ting-a-ling

ding

dang

dong

jingle

jangle

DING

di...

DIN

That afternoon, William rang his bell.
"Sara," he called. "Could you bring me a blanket?"
He rang his bell again.
"Charles! Robert! Can you open the
window? It's too hot now.
John! Will you read me a story?"

DONG DING DIIIING DANG DANG DONG DONG DANG

William rang his bell again.
"What does he want *now*?" said Andrew.
"He wants potato chips," said Louise.
"Who's going to get them?" said Sara;
"it's cold outside and –
look! It's snowing."

"They're very quiet downstairs,"
thought William.
"Where's my lunch?"
He looked out of
the window.

There they were!
Out in the snow.

William waited and waited.
At last Louise came in with a tray.
"Where are my potato chips?" said William.
"Sorry," said Louise,
"but we made rice pudding instead.
It will be better for your throat."

Andrew peeked into the room.
"Come on, Louise. We're ready."
"Ready for *what*?" said William.
"We'll tell you later," said Louise.

William looked at the rice pudding.
Then he looked at his puzzle;
the pieces were all over the bed
and there were crumbs *everywhere*.
"Where *is* everyone?"

CRASH! clatter clatter THUMP.

"What's that?"
He heard the sound of sawing.

screeee-scrawww   screeeee-scrawww

"They're making something!"
said William.

Was it a shelf?
A letterbox? A birdhouse?
. . . a giant birdhouse?

BAM
BAM
BAM
BAM

BANG
BANG **BANG** BOING!

. . . a trampoline?
William jumped out of bed and ran downstairs.

"William! what are you doing out of bed?
Have you seen what we've made?"
William's mouth was too full to answer.
"Come and see," said Sara.

It was a sled!

"Who's going to steer first?"
  said Louise.
"I am," said William.
"But you're sick," said Louise.
"I *was* sick," said William.
"I'm feeling much better now, thank you."

All afternoon they went sledding.

When they got home, William said,
"Tea time."
Everyone was hungry except Louise.
"But there's doughnuts and chocolate
cake," said William.
"I don't want any," said Louise.
"I'm going to bed.
I think I'm sick."